My dearest puppy, Storm,

I hope this letter reaches you safe and sound. You have  had to flee from the

Do not worry a until you are strong enough to return and lead our pack. For now you must move on – you must hide from Shadow and his spies. If Shadow finds this letter I believe he will try to destroy it . . .

Find a good friend – someone to help finish my message to you. Because what I have to say to you is important. What I have to say is this: you must always

Please don't feel lonely. Trust in your friends and all will be well.

Your loving mother,

Canista

Sue Bentley's books for children often include animals, fairies and wildlife. She lives in Northampton and enjoys reading, going to the cinema, relaxing by her garden pond and watching the birds feeding their babies on the lawn. At school she was always getting told off for daydreaming or staring out of the window – but she now realizes that she was storing up ideas for when she became a writer. She has met and owned many cats and dogs and each one has brought a special kind of magic to her life.

Sue Bentley

Sparkling Skates

Illustrated by Angela Swan

PUFFIN

To Honey – such a sweetie and a
friend for only a short time

PUFFIN BOOKS

Published by the Penguin Group
Penguin Books Ltd, 80 Strand, London WC2R 0RL, England
Penguin Group (USA) Inc., 375 Hudson Street, New York, New York 10014, USA
Penguin Group (Canada), 90 Eglinton Avenue East, Suite 700, Toronto, Ontario, Canada M4P 2Y3
(a division of Pearson Penguin Canada Inc.)
Penguin Ireland, 25 St Stephen's Green, Dublin 2, Ireland (a division of Penguin Books Ltd)
Penguin Group (Australia), 250 Camberwell Road, Camberwell, Victoria 3124, Australia
(a division of Pearson Australia Group Pty Ltd)
Penguin Books India Pvt Ltd, 11 Community Centre, Panchsheel Park, New Delhi – 110 017, India
Penguin Group (NZ), 67 Apollo Drive, Rosedale, North Shore 0632, New Zealand
(a division of Pearson New Zealand Ltd)
Penguin Books (South Africa) (Pty) Ltd, 24 Sturdee Avenue, Rosebank,
Johannesburg 2196, South Africa

Penguin Books Ltd, Registered Offices: 80 Strand, London WC2R 0RL, England

puffinbooks.com

First published 2009
4

Text copyright © Sue Bentley, 2009
Illustrations copyright © Angela Swan, 2009
All rights reserved

The moral right of the author and illustrator has been asserted

Set in Bembo
Made and printed in England by Clays Ltd, St Ives plc

British Library Cataloguing in Publication Data
A CIP catalogue record for this book is available from the British Library

ISBN: 978-0-141-32477-7

Prologue

The young silver-grey wolf sped across the ice. Dark clouds were gathering overhead and it began to snow. Storm lifted his head. A big snowflake landed on his nose and he licked it off. It felt good to be back in his homeland.

Suddenly a fierce howl seemed to split the still air.

'Shadow!' Storm gasped. The powerful

lone wolf who had attacked the Moon-claw pack and wounded Storm's mother was very close.

There was a flash of bright golden light and a shower of dazzling sparks. Where the young wolf had been standing there now crouched a tiny puppy with fluffy black fur, a stocky body and short little legs.

Storm scampered forward, his little puppy heart beating fast. He hoped this disguise would protect him from his enemy.

The snow was falling thickly now. It swirled round Storm as he tore towards a thick clump of pine trees. He needed to find somewhere to hide, and quickly. His breath fogged in the cold air as he scrambled into the trees.

A large dark shape moved between the trunks and Storm saw wolf eyes gleaming through the curtain of snow. He caught his breath and skidded to a halt, ready to turn and run away as fast as he could.

'Storm! This way, quickly!' the wolf called in a soft growl.

'Mother.' Storm sighed with relief. He rushed forward and weaved through the trees until he reached the she-wolf.

'It is good to see you again, my son,' Canista rumbled, licking her disguised cub's fluffy black fur and small square muzzle.

Storm yipped a greeting. He wriggled his stocky little body and wagged his stumpy tail as he licked his mother's face. 'I have come back to lead the Moon-claw pack!'

Canista showed her sharp teeth in a proud smile. 'Bravely said, but now is not the time. Shadow still wants to be leader and he is too strong for you. I remain weak from his poisoned bite.'

Storm's midnight-blue eyes narrowed with anger and sorrow. He knew that his mother was right, but he was reluctant to leave her.

'The other wolves will not follow Shadow – they are waiting for you. Go back to the other world. Return when you are stronger and your magic is more powerful.' As Canista finished speaking, her eyes clouded with pain.

Storm leaned close and huffed out a warm puppy breath, which glinted with thousands of tiny gold sparkles. The mist swirled round Canista's injured paw and then disappeared into her grey fur.

Canista gave a sigh of relief as a tiny

bit of her strength returned. But before
Storm could complete the healing,
another terrifying howl rang out,
sounding much closer. Heavy paws
thundered against the ground as a huge
wolf crashed through the trees and Storm
could hear harsh breathing.

'Shadow knows you are here! Go now,
Storm! Save yourself,' Canista urged.

Storm whimpered as dazzling gold
sparks bloomed in his fluffy black fur and
he felt the power surging through him.
The gold glow around him grew brighter.
And brighter . . .

Chapter
ONE

'I can't wait to ask Mum and Dad about having ice-dance lessons!' Lauren Medley said as she and Jemila came out of the White Water ice rink.

'It would be great if you joined the Ice Academy with me!' Jemila said, her dark eyes sparkling. 'We can go to classes together. Maggie, our coach, is great.'

Lauren smiled at her best friend. Jemila

was in the same class at school and was a brilliant ice dancer. She was going to be performing in the show at the rink in a few weeks' time.

'Ice skating's so different to everything else I've ever tried. I love it to bits and I know it's something I really want to do,' Lauren enthused.

Jemila smiled. 'I think Maggie noticed that. She told me that she'd like to meet you sometime.'

'Really? That's fantastic. Here's Mum now. Fingers crossed!' Lauren flicked back her shoulder-length fair hair as she ran over to her parents' car and opened the door. 'Hi, Mum. Is it OK if we give Jemila a lift home?'

Lauren's mum nodded. 'Yes, of course it is. Hop in, you two.'

'Thanks, Mrs Medley,' Jemila said politely as she climbed into the back seat.

'Did you have a nice time at the rink?' Lauren's mum asked her as she drove off.

'The best! I've been practising some new moves. I'm getting really good at skating,' Lauren replied. 'And guess what? Jemila's going to do a solo dance at the ice-dance show!'

'Congratulations!' Mrs Medley smiled at Jemila in the driver's mirror. 'We'll have to get tickets to come and watch you.'

'I really love ice skating and I want to be an ice dancer too, Mum,' Lauren said eagerly. 'So can I join the Ice Academy with Jemila? Some other girls from my class at school are going to join too. And we're all –' She stopped as she saw that her mum was glancing across at her with raised eyebrows.

'So – ice dancing's your latest craze, is it? What happened to BMX biking? You were crackers on that a few months ago,' Mrs Medley commented.

'I know, but this is different. I was rubbish at that other stuff, but I'm good at ice dance! Even Maggie, the coach, thinks I show promise. Isn't that great?' Lauren said eagerly.

'Hmmm.' Her mum rolled her eyes. She drove into a tree-lined road and drew up outside a red-brick house.

'Thanks for the lift. See you at school tomorrow, Lauren!' Jemila called as she got out and went towards her house.

'Bye!' Lauren waved.

As they drove off, Lauren chewed her nails nervously. 'So, when can I start ice-dance classes?' she prompted.

'I'm not sure I'm keen on the idea,' her mum said. 'Let's wait until we get home before we discuss it. I want to see what your dad has to say.'

'OK.' Lauren just about managed not to say anything more. She was feeling hopeful as she followed her mum into their house. Her dad was really easy-going. He was bound to agree to her having lessons.

But she was disappointed this time. 'I'm sorry, but I agree with your mum,' Mr Medley decided after Lauren and her mum had finished talking. 'We've already paid for tennis lessons *and* bought you a BMX bike. It doesn't make sense to shell out for skates and ice-dance lessons when you'll probably lose interest in about five minutes.'

'But I won't! Not this time – honest!' Lauren promised. She knew that she really meant it this time. 'And you won't even have to buy skates. Jemila's promised to give me her old ones!'

'It sounds like you and Jemila have got this all worked out,' her dad said, raising

his eyebrows.

'We have!' she said hopefully, giving him her best pleading smile.

Her dad shook his head slowly. 'Even so, I'm sorry, Lauren, but the answer's the same.'

Lauren knew when she was beaten. She sighed as she trudged out of the room and went upstairs.

'Great! Everyone in my class is joining up. Except me,' she murmured glumly, her spirits sinking. She imagined all the lonely evenings while her friends had fun without her. What she wanted most of all was to pursue her dream of dancing on ice.

Just as Lauren reached the top step there was a dazzling flash of bright gold light and a silent explosion of sparks that lit up the entire landing.

'Oh!' Lauren gasped, rubbing her eyes. When she could see again, she noticed that a tiny fluffy puppy with black fur and a little square muzzle stood there.

'Can you help me, please?' it woofed.

Chapter
TWO

Lauren's jaw dropped and she gaped at
the tiny puppy in complete astonishment.
Was she imagining things?

She rubbed her eyes and looked
again, but the puppy still stood there. It
was gazing up at her with the biggest,
brightest midnight-blue eyes she had ever
seen.

'Where . . . where have you suddenly
come from? How did you get in here?'

Lauren asked, puzzled.

'I used my magic to come here from far away. My name is Storm, of the Moon-claw pack. What is yours?' the puppy yapped softly.

Lauren did a double take. 'Whoa! You really *can* talk! I thought I'd imagined that too!' She swallowed. 'I'm Lauren. Lauren Medley. I live here with my mum and dad.'

Storm bowed his little head. 'I am

honoured to meet you, Lauren.'

'Er . . . me too,' Lauren said, still having trouble taking this all in. As she bent down to make herself seem less big and frightening to this amazing puppy, she remembered something he had said. 'Why do you need my help?'

Storm laid back his ears and his little muzzle wrinkled nervously. 'An evil lone wolf called Shadow is looking for me. He attacked our Moon-claw pack and killed my father and litter brothers and wounded my mother, so that he might lead the wolves. But it is *my* destiny.'

Lauren frowned. 'How can you lead a wolf pack? You're just a tiny pu—'

'Stand back, please,' Storm ordered.

As Lauren stood up and backed slowly into her bedroom there was another dazzling flash of golden light and the tiny black puppy disappeared. In its place, almost filling the entire landing, stood an impressive young wolf with silver-grey fur and a thick neck ruff that twinkled with thousands of lights, like glittering yellow fireflies.

'Storm?' Lauren eyed the powerful wolf's big teeth nervously.

'Yes, it is me. Do not be afraid,' Storm rumbled in a soft velvety growl.

Before Lauren had time to get used to seeing Storm as his true self, there was a final, even brighter flash of light and a fountain of sparks sprinkled down all around Lauren, crackling harmlessly to the carpet.

When Lauren's sight cleared she saw that Storm was a tiny, cute helpless puppy once more. 'Wow! That's a brilliant disguise,' she breathed. 'No one would know that you're not really a cute little Scottie dog.'

'Shadow will know it is me, if he finds me. I need to hide now,' Storm whined.

Lauren saw that the tiny puppy was beginning to tremble all over. She felt a surge of protectiveness and gently picked him up. Storm snuggled into her arms as she stroked his fluffy black fur.

'You can live here with me in my

bedro–' Lauren paused as she realized that there was no way her mum and dad were going to let her have a puppy. They'd just think it was another one of her impulsive madcap ideas, especially after the ice-dance discussion. 'Oh, I don't think you can stay here after all,' she said sadly.

Storm nodded. 'I understand. Thank you for your kindness. I will find someone else to help me.'

But Lauren wasn't ready to lose her new magical friend so quickly. She thought hard. 'Maybe I can hide you in my bedroom. I could make you a bed inside my wardrobe, but you'd need to stay really quiet and not run about or anything when Mum and Dad are in the house. It might be really boring for you, though.'

Storm tipped up his intelligent little

face and blinked at her. 'I would like to stay here in your room. It is a safe place. And I will use my magic, so that only you will be able to see and hear me.'

'You can make yourself invisible? Cool! There's no problem then!' Lauren said eagerly.

She opened her wardrobe and began chucking out old pairs of trainers and a box of old dolls and teddies to make room for a bed for Storm.

'Lauren? I hope you're not too upset about . . . Hello, what are you up to?' asked a surprised voice from the open doorway.

Lauren whipped round to see her mum standing there. In all the excitement of finding Storm, she hadn't heard anyone coming up the stairs. 'I thought I'd . . . er

. . . have a clear-out of . . . um, some old clothes and toys and . . . er, stuff,' she said hastily.

Mrs Medley took a step forward. She put the back of her hand to her forehead and pretended to feel faint. 'You're tidying your room without being asked to? Wonders will never cease, Lauren Medley!'

Lauren gave an anxious grin.

tensed as her mum seemed to look straight at the tiny black puppy who sat on the floor beside her. But when her mum took no notice of Storm she felt herself relax, as she realized that he must have already made himself invisible.

A secret smile crossed Lauren's face. Perhaps she wouldn't be all by herself while everyone else was ice skating with the Academy after all.

Chapter
THREE

Lauren woke early on Monday morning. She'd been having a wonderful dream about gliding gracefully over the ice in pretty white skates and a shimmering costume trimmed with sparkling white feathers.

The feathers were tickling her nose. Lauren lifted a hand to brush them away and then realized that she had her cheek

pressed to Storm's soft fluffy black fur.

She grinned with delight as she
gathered the tiny puppy close for a
cuddle. 'Hello, you,' she crooned. 'Did you
sleep well?'

'Yes, thank you. I feel safe here,' Storm
woofed, lifting his head to lick her chin
with his little pink tongue.

'I'm glad,' Lauren said. 'Because I love
having you living with me.' She told him
all about her dream. 'I was playing the

Sleeping Beauty in a fabulous ice show.
Being a top ice dancer was so amazing!'

Storm put his head on one side, his
dewy eyes bright. 'What is ice dancing?
Winter is very cold in my homeland and
lakes become covered with ice. But we do
not dance on them.'

'It's something people do for fun. We
wear special boots with metal blades
to skate across the ice. But you have to
practise a lot and learn to do jumps and
twists and stuff in time to music to be an
ice dancer,' Lauren explained.

Storm nodded. 'It sounds very exciting.
Are you going to do this?'

'I want to, more than anything. But I
don't think it's going to happen,' Lauren
said, her whole body drooping back
against the duvet.

'Why is that?' Storm's furry little face creased in concern.

'Mum and Dad think that I'll get bored with ice dancing, so they won't pay for me to join the Ice Academy, and be coached, like all my friends. I did used to get fed up with things easily when I was younger,' Lauren explained honestly, 'but I've changed. I know I have. It means everything to me to become an ice dancer. If I could just find some way to prove it, Mum and Dad might change their minds and let me join.'

'Is joining the Ice Academy the only way to get better at ice dancing?' Storm yapped.

'It is really – unless I had my own private ice rink. Then I could practise whenever I wanted to!' Lauren joked glumly. 'But that's never going to happen. So I might as well *totally* give up on the idea. Anyway, that's my hard luck, isn't it? Don't you worry about me, Storm.'

Lauren forced herself to cheer up as she threw back the duvet and jumped out of bed. She was usually a happy person and, after all, she had Storm to keep her company now. 'Time to get up. I've got to get ready for school.'

Storm watched as Lauren began pulling on her school uniform, a thoughtful expression on his little square face.

Lauren smuggled some food upstairs for Storm after she finished her breakfast. She stood by, watching him slurping up the cereal and milk. 'Sorry, but that's all there is for now. I'll get you some proper dog

27

food on my way home from school.'

Storm was licking milk from his chops. 'That was very nice. Thank you.'

Lauren beamed at him. He looked so cute with a white milk moustache on his little black muzzle. It was hard to believe that the tiny helpless puppy was really an impressive young wolf.

'Will you be OK hiding up here while I'm at school?' she asked.

'I will come with you!' Storm yapped, his midnight-blue eyes gleaming.

Lauren wasn't sure if it was a good idea to have a lively puppy bounding around the classroom – even if he was invisible. But Storm looked so eager to come with her that she smiled and gave in. 'Well . . . all right then.'

'Are you ready, Lauren? I'll be in the

car,' her mum called up the stairs.

'OK. Just coming!' Lauren answered.
She turned back to Storm. 'Mum's
dropping me off on her way to work.
Why don't you get in my school bag for
now?'

Storm nodded. Lauren opened her bag
and he immediately jumped in and curled
up next to her purple fake-fur pencil case.

Ten minutes later Lauren stood at the
school gates and waved goodbye as her
mum drove away. 'Here's Jemila. She's my
best friend,' she whispered to Storm as
four girls came walking down the street
towards her and Storm. 'Becky, Katie and
Padmini are all my classmates too.'

'Hi, Lauren. Here are those skates I
promised you,' Jemila said as she reached
Lauren. She handed her a drawstring bag.

Lauren smiled gratefully as she took
the bag. 'Thanks. But I don't think I'll be
needing them now. Mum and Dad won't
let me join the Ice Academy. They reckon
I won't keep it up. I've tried to tell them,
but they won't listen.'

'Oh, poor you. That's rotten,' Jemila said
sympathetically. 'Why don't you keep the

skates anyway, in case they change their minds?'

'And pigs might fly!' Lauren said glumly.

'Bad luck,' said Becky, wrinkling her nose sympathetically.

'Thanks,' Lauren said. Becky was slim with a heart-shaped face and light-brown hair and was very popular in class. Her parents always bought her the latest things and she always looked amazing. But no one minded, as she wasn't at all snooty and was very generous.

'Look! Dad got me the latest copy of *Silver Blades*,' Becky said, taking a glossy magazine out of her bag. 'There are some really cool dance costumes. I'm going to get him to buy me one.'

'Let's see!' Katie and Padmini chorused.

The three of them crowded round the magazine. They chattered excitedly about leotards and the latest designer skates and Lauren gazed longingly at the other girls as they wandered away into the playground.

Jemila hesitated and Lauren could tell that her best friend wanted to join the other girls. She wouldn't have blamed her if she did, but Jemila linked arms with Lauren instead.

Lauren beamed at her friend, pleased that Jemila had chosen to walk into class with her. But she couldn't help thinking sadly about how all four girls would be meeting up in the evenings for lessons at the ice rink, while she stayed at home watching boring TV.

Lauren slipped her hand inside her shoulder bag. Storm woofed softly and immediately began licking her fingers. Lauren began to feel a little bit better, glad that she would have her secret fluffy friend to keep her company now.

Chapter
FOUR

Lauren groaned as she sat looking down at her maths workbook. She didn't seem able to concentrate today and it was taking her ages to work through the exercises. All she could think about was ice skating.

She sat back in her chair. Luckily it wasn't long until the bell went for the end of lessons. Craning her neck, Lauren looked round the room, but there was no sign of Storm.

She wondered what he was up to. Storm had finished exploring the classroom an hour ago and had slipped out to search for other interesting smells to snuffle up.

Just then, Lauren saw a tiny black form squeeze back inside the half-open classroom door. She smiled to herself as the mischievous magical pup scampered towards her between the rows of desks. She was still getting used to the idea that only she could see him and hear him talking.

As soon as Storm reached Lauren, he leapt straight up into the air, trailing invisible sparks behind him like a rocket taking off. He landed – *plonk!* – right on

her maths book.

'Storm! I hope you haven't got mucky paws! Miss will go bananas if I mess up my book!' Lauren whispered, grinning, as she gently lifted him aside.

Storm frowned. He lifted all four paws in turn and examined them, and then nodded, satisfied. 'They are all clean!' he yapped, sitting down beside her. His stumpy little tail began thumping loudly against the desk.

Lauren smothered a giggle and quickly reached out to put her hand over his tail to muffle the sound. But she wasn't quick enough. Becky, who sat directly in front of her, glanced round. She looked puzzled.

'What?' Lauren said innocently.

'I could have sworn I just heard a drum-beat or something,' Becky said. When Lauren looked blank, she shrugged. 'Weird. I must have imagined it.' She turned round again and went back to her work.

Lauren smiled to herself, imagining the look on Becky's face if she told her that an amazing magic puppy was sitting on her desk!

Quickly checking that no one else was looking her way, she whispered to Storm,

'Did you have a good time, finding things to explore?'

Storm nodded, his midnight-blue eyes widening. 'I have just been into a big room with shelves full of lots and lots of books.'

'That's the school library,' Lauren said, wondering why Storm had chosen to spend time in there. 'Didn't you find it a bit boring?'

Storm shook his head, looking very pleased with himself. 'No, it was very interesting!'

Lauren was about to ask him exactly what he had been doing in the library when the bell went.

'All right, class. Tidy up now and put your work away,' the teacher ordered.

There was a sudden noise of chairs

scraping as everyone began getting up
to go home. Lauren stuffed her school
books into her bag and then made space
for Storm to jump inside as well. Picking
up the other bag, which held the skates,
Lauren went outside with Jemila.

As the two of them walked to the
school gates, Lauren saw that her mum
was parked opposite. 'Do you want a lift
home, Jemila?' she offered.

'Thanks, but Becky already asked if I'd
walk home with her. You don't mind, do
you?' Jemila asked.

'No, course not,' Lauren said, although
she did a bit.

'OK, I'll see you in the morning then.'
Jemila jogged towards Becky, who was
waiting a short distance away. Padmini
and Katie hurried forward and joined

them and the four girls walked off together.

Storm was sitting up with his front paws looped over the side of her bag. 'Is something wrong?' he barked as Lauren stared wistfully after her school friends.

'I'm just feeling a bit left out,' Lauren admitted in a whisper. 'All my friends are mad about ice dancing. It's all they talk about. But it's not much use me joining in with them, is it, if I'm not going to lessons with them?'

Storm put his head on one side as he looked up at her. 'I am sorry that you are feeling sad, Lauren.'

Lauren patted one of his soft little paws. 'Thanks, Storm. You're sweet. But I'll just have to get over it, won't I? I'll be fine,' she said softly.

Despite her good intentions about not getting into a bad mood, Lauren sat quietly staring out of the car window on the way home in the car.

Her mum frowned. 'Are you feeling all right, love? You haven't got a tummy ache or headache, have you?'

'No. I'm OK,' Lauren murmured.

'What's that you've got there in that drawstring bag?'

'Jemila's old skates. She said I can keep them, even though there's no chance of

me using them now, is there?' Lauren said,
looking at her mum hopefully.

Her mum gave her a sideways look.
'I hope you're not going to ask about
having ice-dance lessons again. Because
I'm afraid you already know what the
answer will be, don't you?' she said gently.

Lauren sighed and nodded.

The second she got inside the house,
Lauren went into the kitchen to get
herself a drink and grab two bags of crisps
before heading straight upstairs to be by
herself with Storm. He seemed to be the
only one who understood her and she
was really glad that she had him for a
friend.

Her mum looked surprised as Lauren
dashed past. 'Where are you off to in such
a hurry?'

'Got to . . . um, finish some homework!'
Lauren called over her shoulder.

'I'll call you when supper's ready.'

In her bedroom, Lauren put her bag
down and Storm jumped out. They sat
on her bedroom rug together and Lauren
shared her crisps with the tiny puppy.

Storm crunched them all up and then
sat licking his chops. 'Are you ready now?'
he woofed, his big dewy eyes sparkling.

Lauren blinked at him in puzzlement.
'Ready for what?'

Storm didn't answer. Lauren felt a warm tingling sensation flow down her spine as big gold sparks ignited in Storm's fluffy black fur and his little pointed ears fizzled and crackled with miniature lightning flashes.

Excitement glowed through Lauren. It felt like something very strange was about to happen.

Chapter
FIVE

Storm held up one tiny black front paw
and a big spurt of glittering sparkles shot
into the air. Lauren watched in utter
astonishment as the cloud of tiny sparks
whizzed round faster and faster, until
they became like an ice storm inside a
Christmas snow-dome.

The air in front of her shifted like a
shimmering curtain and the room began

to change.

Creak! The walls moved outwards and the room stretched to six times its normal size. *Phut!* The bed, wardrobe and other furniture shrank and lined itself up against one wall. *Crackle!* A small ice rink, with a rail round it, appeared in the centre of the floor.

There was a soft thud and a book appeared on the ground beside her. Lauren bent down to pick it up. The title read *Ice Dance Techniques – Step by Step.*

'Wow! This is amazing!' Lauren exclaimed. She beamed at Storm. Now she knew what he'd been doing in the school library. 'You've thought of everything. Now I can have a practice session. And this book is nearly as good as having a proper coach all to myself!'

'I am glad that you are pleased,' Storm woofed with a toothy little grin.

Lauren couldn't wait to try out the rink. She quickly changed out of her school clothes and put on Jemila's old skates.

'Here I go!' she said delightedly. She took a deep breath and glided on to the ice. It felt amazing to soar along so smoothly that it was almost as if she was flying. Her heart lifted as she knew for certain that this was all she wanted to do from now on.

After five minutes of skating Lauren
had warmed up and was ready to
start work. She picked a simple dance
sequence from the book. After a few
mistakes she had it off by heart and
started practising to make it perfect.

As Lauren became more confident
she felt so happy it was as if her feet
had wings. 'I can't believe how well I'm

doing. You're not using your magic to make me skate better, are you?' she asked suspiciously, zooming past him with her arms outspread.

Storm was sitting at the edge of the rink watching her. He shook his head. 'No, Lauren. I would not do that. It is better for you to learn by yourself. After all, I will not always be here to help you.'

'It must be beginner's luck then . . .' Lauren stopped as Storm's words sank in. She skidded to a halt in a silvery spurt of ice crystals. 'But Shadow won't find you here, will he? So you can live here with me always!'

Storm shook his head slowly and his tiny square face wore a serious expression. 'Shadow will never give up looking for me. And I must one day

return to my home world to lead the
Moon-claw pack,' he reminded her.

Lauren felt a pang. She didn't want to
think about her wonderful little friend
leaving when she'd barely got used to
having him around. 'But that won't be
for a long time yet, will it?' she asked
anxiously.

Storm's little black muzzle wrinkled
in a smile. 'I will stay here for as long as
I can,' he woofed.

'Yay! That's OK then! Watch this!'
Flexing her knees, Lauren shot across the
ice and did a rather squiggly figure of
eight.

'That is very good, Lauren,' Storm
yapped. 'Perhaps I will try ice skating!'
There was another flash of sparks and tiny
gold skates appeared on all four of his

little black paws. Storm zoomed forward
and glided across the ice in a straight line.
But the moment he lifted one front paw,
all the others shot outwards.

'Wur-rooof!' Storm collapsed on to his
tummy in a furry heap.

'Oh dear! Are you all right, Storm?'
Lauren skated over and picked up the
tiny puppy and set him firmly back on
to his paws. Her lips twitched but she bit
back a grin, as she didn't want to hurt her
friend's feelings.

Storm shook himself, flicking powdery ice crystals from his thick black fur. 'It is a lot more difficult than it looks! I think that I will leave ice dancing to you,' he woofed, padding gingerly off the ice. As soon as he stepped on to the bedroom carpet his tiny skates dissolved in a cloud of gold glitter.

An hour later Lauren was hot and sweaty and her legs were aching pleasantly. She glided up to the rail and stepped off the ice. Sitting down next to Storm, she started to remove her skates. 'Phew! That was fantastic. Even Becky hasn't got her very own private skating rink! Thanks, Storm!'

'You are welcome. Now you can practise every night after school,' Storm woofed happily.

Lauren's eyes widened. 'Really? I thought this was a special one-off treat! That's *so* brilliant. I'm going to work hard and get really good. If I can prove to Mum and Dad that I'm serious about being an ice dancer they'll *have* to let me join the Ice Academy!'

'Lauren! Supper's ready!' her mum called upstairs a few minutes later.

'Just coming!' Lauren sang out.

Storm raised his tiny black front paw again and Lauren felt a tingling down her spine as busy magical sparks changed her bedroom back to normal.

Happiness filled Lauren as she and Storm went downstairs together. Storm was the best friend anyone could have.

'How did it go last night?' Lauren asked

Jemila in class the following day. 'Did Padmini, Katie and Becky all sign up for ice-dance classes?'

'Yeah. They all joined. Maggie was really pleased to have some new members. Becky turned up in a brand-new purple leotard and matching skates,' Jemila told her.

Lauren laughed. 'Trust her!'

Jemila laughed too. 'She didn't look too impressed when she saw the uniform we all have to wear – short pleated skirts and T-shirts aren't her style! She said it was like some boring old gym kit! Anyway, it was pretty good fun. But I really wish you could have been there.'

'Me too,' Lauren agreed. She wished that she could tell Jemila about having her own private magic ice rink, but she

knew that she would never give away
Storm's secret — not even to her best
friend.

Lauren darted a secretive glance at
Storm, who was invisibly stretched out
full-length on her desk. He opened one
sleepy midnight-blue eye and his tail
twitched.

'You *are* still coming to the normal
Saturday morning sessions at the rink,

aren't you?' Jemila asked.

Lauren nodded. 'Yes. Mum and Dad are fine about me going to those. And I get my pocket money on Saturdays anyway.'

'Great. We'll all be there as well,' Jemila said. 'We're starting to have classes on Saturdays too. A part of the rink's going to be roped off for the Academy.'

'Is that because of the show in two weeks?' Lauren asked.

'Yes, but Maggie wants us all to work extra hard for the next few weeks. She said the best dancers will be offered a place at summer school.'

'Wow!' Lauren was seriously impressed. Getting a place at ice-dance summer school was beyond even her wildest dreams. She had a thought. 'So you, Becky, Katie and Padmini are all going to be busy behind the roped–off area on Saturday?' She sighed. It looked like she was going to have to skate round all by herself in the public area with loads of kids she didn't know, which wouldn't be nearly as much fun.

'Yeah, but if we all get there early, we can have a normal skate together before class starts in the Academy section,' Jemila said. 'I can show you some of the new moves we've been doing, if you like.'

'I'd love that!' Lauren enthused. *And then with Storm's help I'll be able to practise them in my bedroom every night after school*, she thought.

Chapter
SIX

Lauren usually enjoyed school, but over the next few days she couldn't wait to get home. The second she got back, she shot straight upstairs and spent every spare moment before supper, and an hour or two before bed too, skating on the rink in her magically transformed bedroom.

'I think I'd better have a quiet word with your class teacher,' Lauren's dad decided on Friday evening, when Lauren and Storm came downstairs to get a drink in between ice-dance practice.

Taken by surprise, Lauren blinked at him. 'Why?'

'You've been spending hours upstairs on your homework this past week. Your mum and I have hardly seen you. We're worried that you're having problems with your schoolwork,' he said, looking concerned.

'No! I . . . um, haven't! Everything's fine . . .' Lauren burbled, trying to think of an explanation. It would be seriously embarrassing if her dad came to the school and made a fuss. How was she going to get out of this? She threw a desperate glance at Storm.

Storm pricked his ears and tiny gold

sparks flicked out of the ends. Lauren
heard a thud behind her and turned to
see that the library book was on the floor.

She quickly bent down to pick it up.
'Oops, I . . . um, left it on the chair. I must
have just knocked it off!'

Her dad frowned in surprise as he
reached out and took the book from her.
'What's this? *Ice Dance Techniques*?' he read.

'It's for my . . . er . . . new school
project on ice dance,' Lauren fibbed. 'I
want it to be the best project I've ever
done. That's why I've been spending loads
of time on it. But I didn't tell you about it
because . . .' She had a flash of inspiration.
'. . . because I thought you'd just think I
was trying to get you to let me have ice-
dance classes again,' she finished in a rush.

'Ah, I see.' Her dad gave her a searching
look. 'You're sure this isn't some new
version of pester power?'

'Definitely not!' Lauren said
indignantly. 'But I *am* still mad about ice
dancing, like I said I would be.'

Her dad raised his eyebrows. 'Hmm. It's
still early days. As I remember it, BMX
biking lasted a little while before you
completely lost interest.'

Lauren pulled a wry face. She couldn't deny that. 'This is different, Dad. Just you wait and see!'

'I'll do that,' her dad said, grinning. 'I'd be happy to be proved wrong.' He gave her arm a friendly squeeze before he went out into the garden to cut the grass.

Lauren's shoulder sagged with relief. 'Phew! Thank goodness Dad went for it. I just hope he doesn't ask me to show him my ice-dance project!'

Storm's bright eyes lit up. 'It is no problem if he does!'

There was another small spurt of golden sparkles and Lauren found herself holding a folder. She opened it. It was stuffed full of printed pages and pictures of ice skaters.

'Just in case you will need it,' Storm

yapped.

She gaped at the folder in amazement. 'Where did all this work come from?'

Storm gave her a doggy grin. 'There was a machine in the school library. It had lots of coloured pictures on it. I sat and watched someone using it and saw how they got words and pictures to come out on to paper.'

'You used your magic on a computer? Cool!' Lauren raised her eyebrows.

She smiled at Storm. He was certainly full of surprises. What else could he do?

Lauren was full of high spirits on Saturday morning when her mum dropped her and Storm at the White Water ice rink. Lauren shouldered her red sports bag, with Storm inside it, as she went towards the changing rooms.

She couldn't wait to see Jemila and her other school friends and show them how much her skating had improved.

'It's probably best if you watch from the rink-side seats. It can get crowded on the ice and you might get hurt,' Lauren whispered to Storm as she fastened her skates.

Storm nodded and scampered off to find an empty chair.

Lauren came out of the changing rooms and made her way towards the ice.

'Hi, Lauren!' Jemila called as Lauren glided on to the ice. She was with Padmini, Katie and Becky. They were all wearing their short pleated skirts and matching T-shirts, with 'Ice Academy' in white letters.

Lauren skated over to join her friends.
She felt a bit odd in her ordinary jeans
and plain top. Becky might not like
the uniform, but Lauren would love to
be wearing it. 'Hi, everyone!' she said
brightly.

'Hi, Lauren!'

The girls linked arms and skated round
the rink together for a while. Then Becky,

Pamini and Katie showed Lauren a dance routine they were learning. Lauren began joining in, pleased to be included for once.

'You're really good, Lauren,' Becky said. 'Anyone would think you've been practising as much as we have!'

Lauren grinned to herself. She stood by with her friends as Jemila demonstrated a more complicated dance from the show. She watched closely, admiring the graceful swirls and sweeping movements. Jemila finished off by doing an impressive spin and came to a stop with both arms raised in the air.

'Wow! That was fantastic!' Lauren exclaimed. 'Watch me! I've learned some new moves. I might try and do a spin too!'

'Wait! Be careful . . .' Jemila warned.

But Lauren wasn't listening. She zoomed across the ice to get up speed. All her hours spent skating on her magical secret rink over the past week had given her confidence and she felt as if she could do anything.

As Lauren came out of a long curve she leaned forward and balanced on one leg while raising the other one behind her. Jemila and the other girls cheered. Lauren was enjoying herself so much that she got completely carried away. She took a deep breath and began to go into a twirl.

Lauren spun round faster and faster. Suddenly one skate seemed to slip out from under her. She went over on one ankle, lost her balance and went sprawling backwards.

'Oh!' she gasped as she sat down hard
on her bottom.

Jemila rushed over to help Lauren
get to her feet. 'Are you OK? I tried to
warn you about doing spins. It takes ages
to get them right.'

Lauren dusted powdery ice from her
jeans, her face flaming. 'I'm fine.'

Padmini and Becky were both looking sympathetic.

Katie let out a shout of laughter 'Sorry, Lauren, but you looked so funny. You went down like a sack of potatoes!'

A group of older girls who were standing nearby nudged each other and laughed too. 'Yeah, she did! What a muppet!' one of them mocked.

Lauren ignored them. 'Thanks a lot, Katie,' she murmured, still feeling a bit shaken up.

She felt really silly for showing off in front of her friends, especially as the older girls had been watching too. Lauren realized that she still had a long way to go before she was even half as good as Jemila. Having her own secret ice rink was fantastic, but it would never

be a substitute for belonging to the Ice
Academy.

A slim woman with a pony tail came
on to the ice. She waved and blew a
whistle.

'There's Maggie, our coach. It's time
for our class. We have to go over into the
roped-off area now. Why don't you come
and watch us, Lauren?' Padmini suggested.

'You might pick up a few tips,' Becky
said.

'I think I need to,' Lauren agreed in
a subdued voice. 'I'm just going to get
changed first. I won't be long.' As she
came off the ice and hobbled towards
the changing rooms she saw Storm jump
down from his chair beside the rink.

He pricked up his little black ears as he
came scampering towards her. 'I saw you

slip over. Have you hurt yourself?'

Lauren shook her head. 'No. Just my pride. I'm fine now,' she replied. There was no one else in the changing room as she sat on a bench to take off her skates.

Lauren's red sports bag lay open next to her. Storm leapt straight inside in a whoosh of sparks and curled up.

'Hey! What are you doing with *my* sports bag?' called an annoyed voice.

Lauren looked up to see a girl who looked about thirteen years old coming towards her. It was the ringleader of the older girls who had laughed when she'd fallen over on the ice. She looked tough and unfriendly.

'It's not your bag. It's mine,' Lauren said nervously.

'Yeah, right!' The older girl marched up to the bench, held up her hand and prepared to drop her heavy skates into Lauren's bag – right on top of Storm.

Chapter
SEVEN

There was no time to think. Lauren
moved like lightning. She grabbed her
bag and pulled it towards her, at the same
time thrusting outwards with her free
arm.

'Ow!' Pain crashed through Lauren as
the skates swung against her elbow before
clattering noisily to the floor. But she
tried to ignore it as she made sure that

Storm was all right.

Luckily the tiny puppy had jumped out of the bag when Lauren had grabbed it, and was now standing on the wooden bench. It had happened so fast that Storm looked stunned.

The older girl's eyes glinted with anger as she bent down to pick up her skates. 'Hey! There's no need to take it out on

me, just because you're a pathetic ice-dance wannabe!'

'I didn't . . . I wasn't . . .' Lauren stammered. 'Your skates would have hurt St—' She stopped as she realized that there was no way she could explain about her invisible magical friend. She was struggling to find something to say, when she caught a flash of something red from the corner of her eye. An identical sports bag was hanging from a nearby coat peg.

'Look! That's your red bag!' Lauren said, pointing.

The older girl looked at the bag and her face changed. 'Oh . . . right. Sorry! Gotta go!' She grabbed the red bag, stuffed her skates inside and hurried away.

Lauren crumpled. Now that the danger to Storm was over she felt all wobbly and

her injured arm was throbbing like crazy.
She was glad that no one else had seen
what had happened, and now the other
girl had gone the changing room was
empty again.

Storm seemed to have recovered.
'Thank you for saving me,' he woofed and
then his bright-blue eyes clouded. 'But
you are hurt. I will make you better.'

Lauren felt a familiar warm prickling
sensation down her spine as Storm leaned
forward and huffed out a warm puppy
breath that glowed with thousands of tiny
glittering gold stars. The shimmering mist
surrounded Lauren's arm and she felt a
soothing sensation, just as if cool fingers
were massaging the pain away. It seemed
to run down her arm and flow out of the
ends of her fingers.

'It's much better now. Thanks, Storm.'

Storm jumped on to the floor. 'Shall we go and watch Jemila and the other girls now?'

Lauren nodded. But as she and Storm went back towards the rink she was still smarting with humiliation at having made a fool of herself. She seemed to hear the older girl's words ringing in her head. 'You're just an ice-dance wannabe.'

Maybe I am, Lauren thought glumly. *Maybe all I'll ever be is a wannabe.*

Sunday dawned bright and clear. Lauren and Storm went to a car boot sale with her mum and dad in the afternoon. She was feeling a bit better today, having decided to put what had happened in the changing rooms yesterday behind her. But she couldn't completely forget what the older girl had said.

The old sports ground was bustling with people wandering round the tables full of interesting things. Larger items like furniture, kids' bikes and playpens stood on the grass.

Storm gambolled around invisibly, enjoying all the interesting smells. Lauren could see his furry little black shape dodging between the people wandering about.

When Lauren stopped to look at a stall selling pretty hairslides, Storm dived beneath the table and began nosing about in a box of toys. Moments later he emerged with a hideous bright-pink plastic rabbit held proudly in his mouth.

Lauren almost fell about laughing as

Storm chomped down on the toy with
his sharp puppy teeth.

Squeak! Squeak!

Luckily, with all the noise and activity,
no one had noticed that the squeaky toy
appeared to be floating in mid-air all by
itself. Lauren quickly bent down and held
out her hand. 'Storm! Give it here!' she
whispered.

Storm shook his head, his midnight-blue eyes gleaming mischievously. He wagged his stumpy black tail and bounced down on to his front paws.

'I know you want to play, but you'll have to wait until we get home. There are too many people about here,' Lauren said, trying to sound firm. 'Now, give me that rabbit, please. I'll buy it for you.'

Storm opened his mouth reluctantly and the toy dropped to the grass. Lauren picked it up and paid for it. As she wandered off with Storm at her heels to look at something else, she saw Katie walking towards her.

'Hi!' she called, waving the arm holding Storm's toy.

'What is *that*?' Katie said, laughing, pointing at the bright-pink plastic toy.

'Have you just got a new pet dog or
something?'

Lauren grinned. 'As if! I just . . . er, love
collecting really horrible cheapo toys.
Is Becky with you?' she asked, quickly
changing the subject before she had to
answer any more awkward questions.

'Becky wouldn't be seen dead at a car
booter!' Katie said. 'She's asked Jemila and
Padmini to go and see *The Ice Princess*
with her. I couldn't go because I was
already going out with my mum, but
I thought Becky said she was going to
phone you to ask if you wanted to go
too.'

Lauren would have loved to have
gone to see the film. She couldn't help
wondering whether Becky hadn't
bothered to phone her, now that Lauren

wasn't part of the new ice-dancing gang.

Katie saw the look on Lauren's face.
'You'd probably already left with your
mum and dad by the time Becky phoned,'
she guessed.

Lauren cheered up a bit. That could
be true. Becky might be thoughtless
sometimes, but she wasn't mean.

'Do you fancy getting a burger?' Katie
asked.

At the mention of food Storm barked
eagerly. He jumped up and pawed at
Lauren's leg. 'I like this human food!' he
panted.

Lauren grinned at the tiny puppy's
bright little face and then turned to Katie.
'Why not? The others don't know what
they're missing!'

They bought burgers and wandered

around eating them. Lauren made sure
that Katie didn't notice her breaking off
tiny pieces and dropping them on to the
grass for Storm to gobble up.

After Katie said goodbye and went off
with her mum, Lauren and Storm slowly
made their way back towards her parents'
car, where she'd arranged to meet up with
her mum and dad.

Suddenly Storm gave a yelp of terror
and streaked towards some nearby bushes.

'Storm?' Lauren frowned as she went to
find her little puppy friend.

She reached the bushes and bent down
to peer into the branches. She could see
Storm crouched into a tight ball. His ears
were laid back and he was trembling all
over.

'What's wrong? Are you sick?' she asked
worriedly.

'Shadow has found me. He has put a
spell on those dogs!' Storm whimpered,
his midnight-blue eyes wide and fearful.

'What dogs, Storm?' Lauren looked up
to see a nearby woman with two large
dogs on leads. One of them was barking
excitedly. The woman opened her car
boot and the dogs jumped inside. 'I don't

think those dogs are after you. But how can I tell if they're under a magic spell?' Lauren asked.

Storm burrowed deeper into the hedge. 'They will have fierce pale eyes and extra-large teeth. And be very fierce and strong.'

Lauren looked hard at the dogs in the back of the car as the woman drove slowly past her on the way to the exit. 'Those dogs don't look like that. I think they're normal. Anyway, they've gone now. You can come out.'

Lauren picked Storm up as he crawled out from the bush on wobbly little legs. 'Poor you. You've had a nasty fright,' she whispered, stroking him gently. 'Let's get into our car. Here's Mum and Dad now. We'll soon be home.'

As Lauren sat in the back of the car

with Storm on her lap, she felt his little
heart fluttering against her hand. The
glimpse of possible danger made her
realize all over again that Storm might
have to leave suddenly in order to save
himself.

Lauren felt a pang as she thought that

however much she might try to prepare herself for losing Storm she would never be ready to let him go.

Chapter
EIGHT

A few days later, Lauren was skating round the magical ice rink in her bedroom, after she had helped clear up after supper. Storm sat watching her. He was completely recovered from his fright at the car boot sale and there had been no sign of any of Shadow's dogs.

'Phew!' Lauren panted as she zoomed towards the rail and leaned on it to get her breath back. She felt hot and sticky after practising for an hour and a half. 'I just can't get my head round this new routine. I'm starting to think that I'll never be any good at this.'

Storm wagged his tail encouragingly. 'You are making very good progress, Lauren!'

'Do you really think so?' Lauren smiled at her loyal little friend.

It was really hard to keep practising in secret without any of her classmates to give her encouragement. And, although she had tried to put it behind her, her self-confidence had been shaken by what had happened at the White Water ice rink.

Lauren's damp hair was sticking to her hot face. She wiped it on a towel. 'Maybe I'm just kidding myself. I'll never be good enough to be an ice dancer and Mum and Dad will never let me join the Ice Academy,' she said dejectedly.

Storm's furry black brow wrinkled in a frown. 'But you are getting better all the time. I know how much you love ice dancing and you are working very hard at it. You just have to believe in yourself,

Lauren,' he yapped.

'I know you're right. But that's the hardest part.' Lauren sighed. She was beginning to wonder if she really could do it all by herself – even with Storm's help.

She came off the ice and sat down on her rug to unlace her skates. Storm raised a tiny front paw and glitter swirled around as the ice rink disappeared and her bedroom shrank and became normal.

Lauren got slowly to her feet. Her leg muscles were aching and she felt tired all over.

She could hear the TV on in the sitting room, where her dad sat watching a wildlife programme. Her mum had gone out to the golf course with a couple of her workmates. It was dark outside and

Lauren closed the curtains.

When she turned back into the bedroom Storm was sitting on her bed beside her open ice-dance book. He was resting one tiny front paw on a page and looking closely at a brightly coloured picture.

Lauren bent over to see what he was so interested in. 'That's Naomi Teal in *The Sleeping Beauty on Ice*. She's my favourite dancer. I'd love to be just like her.' She sighed sadly, thinking that she could never be that good. 'I'm going down to say goodnight to Dad and then I'm going to have an early night. Do you want me to let you out into the garden for a quick run first?'

Storm nodded and followed her out.

*

Lauren put on her nightdress and then jumped into bed. She was just settling down with Storm cuddled up in the crook of her arm when she felt a familiar warm prickling sensation down her spine.

'Storm? What are you up to?' she yawned.

Storm's midnight-blue eyes glowed like jewels in the dark as his fluffy black fur ignited with dazzling gold sparks and his ears and tail crackled with electricity.

The bed began to shake and a golden glow appeared around her. Lauren's eyes shot open and she sat upright, suddenly wide awake.

Woo-oosh! Shimmering pillars of light stretched upwards around her and joined together to form ornate walls and a door of golden metal and glass. *Rustle!* Lauren found herself wrapped in feather-soft blankets and sitting on soft cushions inside a fabulous coach. *Jingle!* A team of magnificent white horses was harnessed to the front.

The next instant the horses leapt upwards in a multicoloured spray of sparks. The golden coach zoomed straight *through* the ceiling and sped across the night sky, which was pricked by millions of bright stars.

Lauren was transfixed with wonder.
'Where are we going?' she gasped.

'Wait and see!' Storm woofed
mysteriously. He sat in her lap and she
held his warm little body close as they
streaked onwards. It seemed like no
time at all before the horses' hooves
were skimming across snow-covered
treetops and then the coach was speeding
downwards towards a frozen lake.

'Wow! There's a show on!' Lauren
gasped as she saw the brightly coloured

lights and the ice dancers' beautiful sparkling costumes. An ice castle with turrets and towers, which was lit from within with candles, glowed like a giant, flickering jewel.

A big crowd of people was watching the dancers, while others were strolling around stalls that were set out around the lake's edges. The golden coach landed on a deserted strip of narrow land on the far shore. No one paid any attention and Lauren realized that they must be invisible.

She had a brilliant view from here and leaned forward from inside the warm coach to watch the dancers as they swirled and skimmed across the ice.

'This is like something from a fairytale. Those dancers are amazing!' Lauren enthused. Her breath fogged in the frosty air, but Storm's magic stopped her from feeling the slightest bit cold. Suddenly Lauren spotted a face she recognized. 'I can't believe it! That's Naomi Teal!'

'I know,' Storm woofed, looking very pleased with himself.

Lauren watched the show for the next hour and a half, lost in the wonder of the whole spectacle. This was the best night of her life! As the glittering performance came to an end, the dancers took their bows and the audience's cheers rang out across the lake.

There was a golden flash and the coach and horses rose into the air in another swirling snowstorm of sparks as the horses drew them homewards. With a final fizzle of light and a loud *Pop!* the coach and

horses dissolved and Lauren found herself
back in bed.

'That was so amazing. Thanks, Storm!
I'll never forget this night!'

Storm's little black muzzle wrinkled in
a smile. 'You are welcome.'

'I wish I could dance like that,' Lauren
murmured, stifling a yawn.

Storm looked up at her and placed one
tiny front paw on her cheek. 'You will
one day, Lauren.'

'Do you really think so?' Lauren asked,
looking down into his little face.

Storm nodded. 'Yes, I do. But you will
have to be very determined and hold on
to your dreams. And you must not let
setbacks get you down.'

Just like you, Lauren thought, feeling
proud of her brave little friend who was

determined one day to lead the Moon-
claw wolf pack, despite the danger from
Shadow.

Her heart seemed to swell with new
purpose.

'You're right, Storm. From now on,
I'm going to work *extra* hard. I'll practise
on my magical rink every moment I can
and nothing is going to make me stop!'
If Storm believed in her, she could do it!
She stroked the top of the tiny puppy's
soft little head. 'What would I do without
you?' she whispered sleepily as she
snuggled under the cosy duvet.

Chapter
NINE

Lauren kept her promise to herself and over the following ten days she threw herself into ice-dancing practice with renewed enthusiasm. The time seemed to fly by and then it was the day before the show.

'It's the final dress rehearsal tonight,' Jemila told Lauren nervously after school. 'You wouldn't come with me, would you?'

'Me?' Lauren said, surprised. 'What about Katie, Becky and Padmini, won't they be there?'

Jemila screwed up her nose. 'Yeah, but it's not the same. You're my best friend.'

Lauren smiled. 'Course I'll come! I'd love to.'

'Great.' Jemila beamed at her. 'I'll meet you outside the rink. It's closed, except for dancers or people working on the show, but I know Maggie won't mind. She said we always need extra helpers.

Besides, I've told her all about how you would love to be an ice dancer.'

'Have you?' Lauren said, amazed that Jemila had spoken to the ice-dance coach about her. 'What did she say?'

'Maggie thought it was a shame that your parents wouldn't let you join the Ice Academy when you were so keen. Anyway, bring your skates. You should be able to grab a free go on the ice when we have a break in rehearsals.'

'OK. Sounds great.' Lauren smiled, feeling excited already. 'See you there.'

'Well, I have to say that you do seem to be sticking with ice dancing,' Lauren's dad commented as she and Storm got out of the car in front of the rink later that evening. 'Maybe it's third time lucky then.'

'It is!' Lauren exclaimed. She waved to Jemila, who was waiting for her at the ice-rink entrance. She bent down to smile in through the passenger window at her dad. 'So does that mean you'll let me join the Ice Academy?' she asked cheekily.

'Hmm. We'll see,' he said, smiling. 'See you later.'

'Did you hear that?' Lauren whispered to Storm excitedly as her dad drove away. 'I really think I might be allowed to join soon!'

Storm was sitting with his paws looped over her sports bag. He twisted his head round to look up at her. 'That is good!'

Lauren ruffled the soft fur on his little head. 'Thank you for making me realize that my dream about being an ice skater could come true if I didn't give up. I know now that I'm never, ever going to stop!' she said.

Storm wagged his stumpy black tail.

Lauren and Storm went inside the rink with Jemila. The whole place was transformed. The rink was strung with fairy lights, plastic icicles and flowing white ribbons. Painted cardboard scenery made it into a magical winter forest, with snowy hills and a white castle glistening in the distance.

'Wow! Look at this!' Lauren said. It made her think of her wonderful night-journey across the starry sky to the show on the frozen lake.

But Jemila seemed too nervous to reply. Lauren went into the changing rooms with her. Becky, Padmini and Katie were already there and changing into their costumes. They were going to do a simple dance as forest animals.

As Lauren was helping Jemila into her glittering white costume and matching skates, Maggie came in. The coach had her hair tied back in a pony tail.

Maggie greeted all the girls and gave Lauren a friendly smile before ushering everyone outside to begin the rehearsal.

For the next hour Lauren helped out where she could and then kept out of the way while Maggie put the dancers through their paces. Lauren felt her feet twitching to join in as she watched the girls skating round the ice. She clapped enthusiastically as they performed routine after routine.

'One day, eh?' she whispered to Storm, who sat beside her.

Storm nodded vigorously, his tail twirling.

'Take twenty, everyone!' Maggie called. She led the way off the ice and all the young dancers went to get drinks and relax for a while.

Jemila came over to Lauren. 'Why don't you find a quiet bit of the rink and have a skate? No one will mind.'

'OK.' Lauren didn't need telling twice.

She quickly put on her skates and
glided on to the ice. As music flooded out
over the sound system Lauren lost herself
and danced for pure joy. She was so
engrossed in the ice-dance routine, which
she'd learned by heart, that she didn't
notice the little puff of gold sparkles that
fizzed into the air above where Storm
was sitting watching. A spotlight began
following Lauren across the ice.

Lauren skated on in a world of her own. As she finally swept to a graceful halt she heard clapping.

'Bravo!' called a voice.

Startled, Lauren whipped round to see Maggie walking across the ice towards her. She felt herself going bright red.

'Well done, Lauren! Jemila told me you were good, but I wanted to see for myself,' Maggie said. 'And there you were, caught in the spotlight, so I couldn't help but notice you. How lucky was that? How would you like to come to summer school?'

'Really? I'd love to!' Lauren burst out delightedly. 'But how can I? I don't belong to the Ice Academy.'

Maggie smiled warmly. 'We'll see about that. You leave it to me.'

Lauren left the ice in a daze. She couldn't wait to tell Storm her wonderful news. But as she walked towards him he jumped down and shot towards a storeroom.

Lauren headed for a large piece of scenery that was propped beside the open storeroom doorway, almost blocking off the inside. Suddenly she heard a fierce growling. Dark shapes were prowling along the corridor, coming closer. The lights gleamed on their cold pale eyes and their extra-long teeth.

Lauren's blood ran cold. Shadow's dogs! Storm was in terrible danger.

She dashed round the scenery and squeezed into the storeroom, just as there was a dazzling flash of bright golden light, which lit up the entire room. Storm stood there, a tiny helpless puppy no longer, but his true majestic self: a handsome young silver-grey wolf with a sparkling neck ruff and glowing midnight-blue eyes. An older wolf with a gentle face, whom Lauren guessed was his mother, stood next to him.

And then Lauren knew that Storm was leaving for good. She was going to have

to be very brave. She rushed over and the huge wolf allowed her to hug him one last time.

'I'll never forget you, Storm,' Lauren said, her voice breaking as she buried her face in his thick soft fur.

'You have been a very good friend, Lauren. I will always remember you,' Storm said in a deep velvety growl.

Lauren took a step back just as an ugly snarl sounded right outside, beside the scenery. 'Go. Save yourself, Storm!' she urged in a choked voice.

There was a final flash of light and a silent explosion of bright gold sparks that drifted down around Lauren and fizzled out harmlessly on the storeroom floor. Storm and his mother faded and then were gone. The growl was abruptly cut off and silence fell.

Lauren stood there, her heart aching with sadness. She was going to miss Storm terribly, but at least she knew he was safe. And she would always have her secret memories of the wonderful adventure they'd shared.

'Lauren? Where are you?' called Jemila's voice from the corridor. 'Your dad's looking for you. Maggie's just been talking to him and he's smiling all over his face!'

'Coming!' Lauren called. She brushed away a tear as she went out with new hope in her heart. 'Thanks, Storm, for helping to make my dreams come true! I really hope yours come true too,' she whispered.

Magic Ponies

Could you be a little pony's special friend?

puffin.co.uk

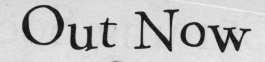

Out Now
Magic Puppy

A little puppy, a sprinkling of magic, a forever friend

Magic Puppy

Sunshine Shimmers

SUE BENTLEY

puffin.co.uk

Coming Soon

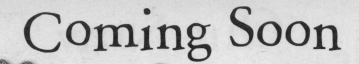

Spellbound at School   **The Perfect Secret**

Magic Puppy

A New Beginning
9780141323503

Muddy Paws
9780141323510

Cloud Capers
9780141323527

Star of the Show
9780141323534

Party Dreams
9780141323794

A Forest Charm
9780141323800

Twirling Tails
9780141323817

School of Mischief
9780141323824

Snowy Wishes
* 9780141323831

Classroom Princess
9780141324791

Friendship Forever
9780141324784

Sparkling Skates
9780141324777

Sunshine Shimmers
9780141324760

Spellbound at School
9780141324753

Coming Soon

The Perfect Secret
9780141324746

A little puppy
a sprinkling of magic,
a forever friend

puffin.co.uk

If you like
Magic Puppy,
you'll love

Magic Kitten

A Summer Spell
9780141320144

Classroom Chaos
9780141320151

Star Dreams
9780141320168

Double Trouble
9780141320175

Moonlight Mischief
9780141321530

A Circus Wish
9780141321547

Sparkling Steps
9780141321554

A Glittering Gallop
9780141321561

Seaside Mystery
9780141321981

Firelight Friends
9780141321998

A Shimmering Splash
9780141322001

A Puzzle of Paws
9780141322018

A Christmas Surprise
9780141323237

Picture Perfect
9780141323480

A Splash of Forever
9780141323497

Magic Puppy

Win a Magic Puppy goody bag!

The evil wolf Shadow has ripped out part of Storm's
letter from his mother and hidden the words so that magic puppy
Storm can't find them.

Storm needs your help!

Two words have been hidden in secret bones in *Sparkling Skates*.
Find the hidden words and put them
together to complete the message from Storm's mother.
Send it in to us and each month we will put every correct message
in a draw and pick out one lucky winner, who will receive
a Magic Puppy gift – definitely worth barking about!

Send the hidden message, your name and address on a postcard to:
Magic Puppy Competition
Puffin Books
80 Strand
London WC2R 0RL
Good luck!

puffin.co.uk

It all started with a Scarecrow

Puffin is well over sixty years old.
Sounds ancient, doesn't it? But Puffin has never been
so lively. We're always on the lookout for the next big
idea, which is how it began all those years ago.

Penguin Books was a big idea from the mind of
a man called Allen Lane, who in 1935 invented
the quality paperback and changed the world.
**And from great Penguins, great Puffins grew,
changing the face of children's books forever.**

The first four Puffin Picture Books were hatched in 1940 and the
first Puffin story book featured a man with broomstick arms called
Worzel Gummidge. In 1967 Kaye Webb, Puffin Editor, started the
Puffin Club, promising to **'make children into readers'.**
She kept that promise and over 200,000 children became
devoted Puffineers through their quarterly installments of
Puffin Post, which is now back for a new generation.

Many years from now, we hope you'll look back and
remember Puffin with a smile. **No matter what your age
or what you're into, there's a Puffin for everyone.**
The possibilities are endless, but one thing is for sure:
whether it's a picture book or a paperback, a sticker book
or a hardback, **if it's got that little Puffin
on it – it's bound to be good.**